STRANGE BEDFELLOWS

Based on the TV series created by
JOSS WHEDON & DAVID GREENWALT.

The book you hold in your hands is the final collection derived from the first *Angel* series published by Dark Horse Comics. The book ran seventeen issues, and here you have stories from the fourth and seventeenth issues, with a little something extra about vampire hookers tossed in the middle. Christopher Golden, later joined by his writing partner Tom Sniegoski, was there from the very beginning with *Angel*, writing the first miniseries—collected as *The Hollower*—through these stories. He followed the gradual evolution of the TV series in that first year. Doyle makes a brief appearance in "The Changeling Wife," but was long dead by the time our titular story, "Strange Bedfellows," rolled around. The last story in this book includes another dead guy—Phantom Dennis, making his first appearance, as it were, in the comics.

The regular artist on the series, Christian Zanier, really got to strut his stuff on the title story, as he's maybe best known for drawing the ladies, scantily clad and otherwise. Christian drew twelve of those original seventeen issues of *Angel*, and the rest were drawn by Eric Powell, making him disproportionately represented in this volume. Covers, more often than not, were drawn by Jeff Matsuda, including the *Pretty Woman* homage featured on the back cover of this book.

Developing a comics series in the shadow of a popular TV show involves evolution on two levels. We had to develop a comic we believed in, while watching as the show searched for its own direction. (When Golden and Zanier were writing and drawing issue one of *Angel*, we still hadn't seen a final draft of the show's debut script.) With the stories in *Strange Bedfellows*, Golden & co. run a gamut of emotions preying on fear, attraction, humor, and revulsion, tending towards the dark heart of what Joss Whedon and David Greenwalt laid out in their first year of shows. Enjoy.

Scott Stuart Allie

publisher

Mike Richardson

editor

Scott Allie

with Mike Carriglitto

collection designer

Keith Wood

art director

Mark Cox

Special thanks to

Debbie Olshan at Fox Licensing.

Published by

Titan Books

144 Southwark Street

London SE1 0UP

First edition: April 2002

ISBN: 1-84023-453-9

2 4 6 8 10 9 7 5 3 1

Printed in Italy.

These stories take place during Angel's first season.

THE CHANGELING WIFE

story
CHRISTOPHER GOLDEN

art
ERIC POWELL

letters
PAT BROSSEAU

colors
GUY MAJOR

JEFF MATSUDA with ANDY OWENS and GUY MAJOR

IF YOU LOOK HARD ENOUGH, YOU CAN FIND ANYTHING IN LOS ANGELES.
ANYTHING.
BITE ME.
WHAT DID YOU SAY?
UH, WELL... ON THE PHONE, THEY SAID YOU...Y'KNOW, THAT YOU WERE INTO THIS STUFF, VAMPIRE FETISHES AND STUFF. THAT IT WAS YOUR SPECIALITY. I ASKED, AND--
SSSH, BABY, IT'S OKAY. THEY'RE RIGHT. I JUST WANTED TO HEAR YOU SAY IT AGAIN.
BITE ME.
OH, YEAH.
I'M YOURS.

IT'S TRUE WHAT THEY SAY. YOU NEVER KNOW WHAT KIND OF VERMIN YOU'RE GONNA FIND DOWN BY THE DOCKS.
GRRAWWRR! LET ME GO, YOU SON OF A--
I DON'T THINK SO.
WHAT THE HELL'S THE MATTER WITH YOU? YOU CRAZY OR SOMETHING? YOU CAN'T JUST--
A LESSON FOR YOU, FRIEND. SOME-TIMES THERE REALLY IS TRUTH IN AD-VERTISING.
HEY, WHERE'D SHE GO?

HIS NAME IS ANGEL. HE HELPS PEOPLE WHO NEED IT.
THEY AREN'T ALWAYS GRATEFUL.
THEN AGAIN, HE ISN'T REALLY DOING IT FOR THEM.
WITHIN HIM LIES A CONSTANT STRUGGLE BETWEEN HIS HUMAN SOUL, AND THE DEMON WHICH ENTERED HIS FLESH WHEN HE BECAME A VAMPIRE.
HE IS DETERMINED THAT THE HUMAN SIDE OF HIM WILL WIN THAT STRUGGLE. TO THAT END, HE WALKS AMONG MORTAL HUMANS, COMING TO THEIR AID WHEN DARKNESS THREATENS.
HIS REWARD IS NOTHING MORE THAN THEIR COMPANY. BEING AROUND THEM, HE HOPES, WILL HELP HIM HANG ONTO WHAT REMAINS OF HIS HUMANITY.
"IN EACH OF US, TWO NATURES ARE AT WAR-- THE GOOD AND THE EVIL. ALL OUR LIVES THE FIGHT GOES ON BETWEEN THEM, AND ONE OF THEM MUST CONQUER. BUT IN OUR OWN HANDS LIES THE POWER TO CHOOSE--WHAT WE WANT MOST TO BE, WE ARE" --ROBERT LOUIS STEVENSON.

OF COURSE, SOMETIMES-- AS IN THE CASE OF THE MORON WHO VOLUNTEERED TO BE BITTEN BY A VAMPIRE-- HE'S FORCED TO WONDER IF THAT'S REALLY A GOOD THING.
THAT KIND OF THINKING GETS HIM FEELING KINDA ANTI-SOCIAL.

--DONE WITH YOU! YOU'RE A MONSTER! ALL YOU WANT IS TO TEAR ME DOWN, TO DESTROY ME! I LOST MY JOB, WE'RE GONNA LOSE THE HOUSE--
AND IT'S A
BECAUSE
YOU!
SLAP!

YOU'VE DESTROYED MY LIFE. I HOPE YOU'RE HAPPY NOW.
I HOPE IT WAS WORTH IT TO YOU. I HOPE IT WAS WORTH *THIS!*

THAT'LL DO.
CALL THE POLICE. QUICKLY!
NO.
BACK OFF, BUDDY. YOU DON'T KNOW WHAT YOU'RE GETTING IN THE MIDDLE OF. YOU THINK THIS IS MY WIFE, RIGHT?
UH-UH. SHE'S NOT EVEN HUMAN!
DON'T TALK TO ME ABOUT HUMAN, MISTER. NOT AFTER WHAT YOU WERE ABOUT TO DO.
YEAARRGHH!
STOP! YOU DON'T UNDER-STAND. SHE'S NOT CASSIE. SHE'S SOME KIND OF DEMON OR SOME-THING. SHE'S POISONING MY LIFE.

YOU'RE OUT OF YOUR MIND. AND YOU NEED SOME SERIOUS HELP. BUT FIRST... APOLOGIZE.
IT'S ALL RIGHT. REALLY. PLEASE LET HIM GO.
ALL RIGHT? HE'S DELUSIONAL. HE WAS GOING TO--
PLEASE.
IT'S ALL RIGHT, ROB. IT'LL BE ALL RIGHT NOW. YOU'LL SEE.
THAT'S HIM, OFFICERS. MR. KOENIG.
WHAT'S WRONG WITH YOU? WHY DID YOU HAVE TO INTERFERE?
HE WAS ABOUT TO BASH YOUR BRAINS IN WITH A CHAIR. I THOUGHT YOU NEEDED HELP. AND I'M NOT THE ONLY ONE, OR THE COPS WOULDN'T HAVE ARRESTED HIM.
I WON'T BE PRESSING CHARGES. MAYBE NEXT TIME, YOU'LL MIND YOUR OWN BUSINESS.
DON'T TEMPT ME.

I'M TELLIN' YA, LOCKLEY, YA GOTTA GET OUT MORE. YA CAN'T MAKE THE JOB YOUR LIFE.
TAKE ME, FER INSTANCE. I USED TA BE MISERABLE BE- FORE I STARTED MEETING NEW PEOPLE.
YEAH, JENKINS. YOU'RE A REAL SOCIAL BUTTERFLY. I'LL BE RIGHT BACK. I NEED COFFEE.
MEET NEW PEOPLE. RIGHT. LIFE IS COMPLICATED ENOUGH.
NO ARGUMENT HERE.

WHAT ARE YOU DOING HERE?
LITTLE WHILE AGO, I STOPPED A GUY NAMED ROB KOENIG FROM BEATING ON HIS WIFE WITH A METAL CHAIR. SHE WAS ANGRY THAT I'D GOTTEN IN-VOLVED. I HAVE A HARD TIME UN-DERSTANDING THAT.
A PSYCHIATRIST COULD TELL YOU WHY. ALL I KNOW IS WHAT I SEE. A LOT OF ABUSED WOMEN NEVER LEAVE THE GUY, NEVER EVEN PRESS CHARGES.
SO THAT'S IT? THANKS FOR YOUR HELP.
BELIEVE ME, I'D LOVE TO LOCK UP EVERY ABUSIVE HUSBAND I COME ACROSS. BUT WITH-OUT THE WOMAN'S COOPERATION, THERE ISN'T MUCH YOU CAN DO.
NOTHING *YOU* CAN DO, MAYBE. BUT I DON'T THINK KOENIG'S DONE WITH HIS WIFE. NOT BY A LONG SHOT.
AND I'M NOT JUST GOING TO STAND BY AND WATCH IT HAPPEN.

KRASH!

GIVE ME THAT.
YOU? BUDDY YOU'RE MAKING A BIG MISTAKE. YOU'RE ON MY PROPERTY. I'M GONNA--
YOUR HOME. YOU'RE WIFE DIDN'T PRESS CHARGES. I JUST WANTED TO MAKE SURE YOU DIDN'T THINK THAT WAS PERMISSION TO HURT HER.

I'LL BE WATCHING.

YOU DO THAT, PAL. YOU CAN'T STOP ME. NOBODY CAN.

WHY DON'T YOU MIND YOUR OWN BUSINESS? YOU HAVE NO IDEA WHAT YOU'RE GETTING INVOLVED WITH HERE.

HUH. NO I GUESS I DON'T

GOD, WHERE'S ROSENBERG WHEN YOU COULD USE HER HACKING SKILLS?
STARBUCKS
MORNING, CORDELIA. I THOUGHT I'D PICK US BOTH UP SOME--
DOYLE. YOU LOOK LIKE SOME-THING THE CAT WOULD REFUSE TO DRAG IN.
NO WONDER YOU'RE WILLING TO DRINK WHAT PASSES FOR COFFEE DOWN AT THAT SLEAZY DINER.

WELL, I GUESS IT'S THE THOUGHT THAT COUNTS.
IF IT HELPS YOU TO BELIEVE THAT...
SO, WHAT ARE WE WORKING ON?
ANGEL LEFT A NOTE. WE'RE TRACKING DOWN NEWS ITEMS OR POLICE RECORDS ON THIS GUY, ROBERT KOENIG.
GREAT. WE'LL BE AT THIS ALL BLOODY DAY.
LATER.
SO, HOW'D IT GO?
THRILL A MINUTE. WHICH WAS GOOD, CONSIDERING IT WAS MANY, MANY LONG AND HELLISH MINUTES. HOURS. HAS IT BEEN A WHOLE YEAR?
THIS KOENIG GUY IS BAD NEWS. TURNS OUT HE'S BEEN ARRESTED FOUR TIMES. TWICE FOR ASSAULTING HIS WIFE, AND A COUPLE OF OTHER TIMES WITH OLD GIRL-FRIENDS.
I DON'T KNOW. I GOT A STRANGE VIBE FROM HIS WIFE THE OTHER NIGHT.
WAIT, YOU DON'T ACTUALLY BELIEVE THIS NUT-JOB? PLEASE. EVEN IF HIS WIFE WAS SOME KIND OF DEMON, THAT DOESN'T EXPLAIN THE OTHER ARRESTS.
DESPITE WHAT SOME MEN THINK, NOT ALL WOMEN ARE RAVING HELL-BEASTS. SOME-BODY'S GOT TO STOP THE JERK BEFORE HIS WIFE ENDS UP DEAD.
OH, KOENIG'S DANGEROUS. YOU'LL GET NO ARGUMENT ON THAT FROM ME.

"BUT I'M NOT SURE HE'S THE ONLY ONE.

"I MAY NOT BE QUITE SURE WHAT'S GOING ON HERE. BUT I'M GOING TO FIND OUT, ONE WAY OR ANOTHER."

WHERE DO YOU THINK YOU'RE GOING, KOENIG?

N VACATION. OT THAT IT'S NY OF YOUR-- EY! WHAT ARE YOU DOING?
I WANT TO TALK TO YOUR WIFE. WHERE IS SHE?

GET OFF MY PROPERTY! I'LL--I'LL CALL THE POLICE.
FEEL FREE. IN THE MEAN-TIME, GET OUT OF MY WAY.

I-I MEAN, YOU CAN'T...
STEP ASIDE. NOW.
BOOM!

CASSIE! MRS. KOENIG! OPEN THE DOOR!

I HOPE YOU BURN ALONG WITH HER, YOU CRAZY FREAK.

KRUNCH!!
AAARRGH!
STOP. IT'S NOT WHAT YOU THINK. THAT'S NOT CASSIE UP THERE, NOT MY WIFE. IT'S SOME KIND OF MONSTER. IT LIVES JUST TO TORMENT ME. IT'S THE TRUTH.
AYBE IT IS. BUT ST IN CASE, I'M NOT GOING TO T HER BURN TO ATH. OPEN THE DOOR. NOW!
OKAY! OKAY! I DON'T KNOW WHY YOU DON'T JUST BREAK IT DOWN.
GUESS I'M JUST POLITE.
YOU'RE CRAZY! MAYBE YOU WANT TO BURN TO DEATH WITH HER, BUT I'M NOT--
SWACK!

CASSIE!
KRAK!

CRUNCH
HANG ON. I'LL GET YOU OUT OF HERE.

AYBE YOU ON'T MIND THE HELP HIS TIME.
THANK YOU... KAFF-KAFF ...SO MUCH. I NEVER... KAFF-KAFF ...NEVER THOUGHT HE WOULD GO THIS FAR.

IT'S OKAY. YOU'RE GOING TO BE ALL RIGHT NOW.

OH, ROB!
COME ON! I'LL COME BACK IN FOR HIM!

NO, NO...
I'LL TAKE CARE OF DEAR ROBERT.
I INSIST.
THE MAN SPOKE THE TRUTH, VAMPIRE, BUT ONLY PART OF IT. I AM A CHANGE-LING, DAUGHTER OF THE FEY QUEENS, THE TUATHA DE DANANN.
ALL HIS LIFE, THIS ONE HAS TAKEN PLEASUR IN CAUSING WOMEN PAIN. WHEN IT BECAM TOO MUCH FOR CASS SHE CALLED ON MY MISTRESSES FOR HEL THEY REMOVED HE TO A BETTER PLACE.
...AND LEFT ME IN HER PLACE. SHE LIVES AMONG THEM NOW, UNTIL I HAVE FULFILLED MY PURPOSE. UNTIL ROBERT KOENIG IS PUNISHED.
NO.

YOU DARE? AFTER WHAT THIS MAN HAS DONE, THE AGONY HE HAS INFLICTED? I SENSE THE HUMAN SOUL IN YOU, CREATURE, JUST AS I SENSE THE DEMON.
WHICH OF THEM, I WONDER, WOULD DEFEND THIS MONSTER OF A MAN?.
YOU WERE RIGHT, ROBERT. I WAS HERE TO HURT YOU. TORMENT YOU. DESTROY YOU. BUT I WASN'T TO KILL YOU UNTIL I'D DRIVEN YOU MAD.
LET'S SEE IF WE CAN'T ACCOMPLISH THAT ***NOW.***
SWAKK!

YOU WOULD DIE TO KEEP ME FROM KILLING A DEPRAVED BEAST SUCH AS THIS?
HIS DEATH ISN'T FOR EITHER OF US TO DECIDE. HE'S EVERY-THING YOU SAY HE IS--TRUST ME, I KNOW ABOUT DEPRAVITY, AND WHAT IT MEANS TO BE A BEAST--BUT HIS FATE'S FOR THE AUTHORITIES TO DECIDE.
MY MISTRESSES ARE THE REAL AUTHORITY HERE.
YOU'RE WRONG ABOUT THAT.
AND YOU'RE WRONG ABOUT ONE OTHER THING...

I DON'T NEED TO DIE TO STOP YOU FROM KILLING.
THIS IS NOT YOUR WORLD. YOUR MISTRESSES--WHOEVER THEY ARE--HAVE NO AUTHORITY HERE. KOENIG WILL BE PUNISHED ON HUMAN TERMS.
BUT YOU AND I? WE'RE BOTH CREA-TURES OF DARK-NESS.
IN OUR WORLD, THERE'S REALLY ONLY ONE WAY FOR THINGS TO END.
NO...
LET YOUR MISTRESSES SAVE YOU IF THEY WILL.
WHEE-OOO!

"SO KOENIG ISN'T GOING TO STAND TRIAL?"
NOT A CHANCE. HIS MIND IS GONE, I GUESS THE CHANGE-LING GOT HER JOB DONE AFTER ALL.
YOU REALLY BELIEVE THAT, THEN? THAT SHE WAS A CHANGE-LING, SENT DOWN BY THE FAERIES?
I'M NOT SURE WHAT TO BELIEVE. THE POLICE DIDN'T FIND A BODY. MAYBE THE FEY QUEENS SAVED HER AFTER ALL.
GUYS, COME ON. VAMPIRES, DEMONS, OKAY. BUT ARE WE SAYING WE BELIEVE IN FAERIES, NOW?
GUYS?
"THE WORLD IS FULL OF WEIRD THINGS, CORDELIA.
"EVENTUALLY, THEY ALL FIND THEIR WAY TO LOS ANGELES."
End

ANGEL™

STRANGE BEDFELLOWS

story
CHRISTOPHER GOLDEN
& TOM SNIEGOSKI

pencils
CHRISTIAN ZANIER
with MARVIN MARIANO

inks
ANDY OWENS
& DEREK FRIDOLFS

letters
CLEM ROBINS

colors
LEE LOUGHRIDGE

CHRISTIAN ZANIER
with DAN JACKSON

LOS ANGELES, CALIFORNIA IS RENOWNED FOR ITS PERVERSIONS AND PECCADILLOES. HERE, SCANDAL IS A WAY OF LIFE.
ON THE AVERAGE L.A. MORNING, RUINOUS GOSSIP IS CONSUMED WITH MORE FREQUENCY AND IN MORE VOLUME THAN ORANGE JUICE OR BREAKFAST CEREAL.
SLEEPYTIM MOTOR LODGE
YOU GOT THE RUN DOWN, RIGHT, HONEY? PETRA TOLD YOU HOW IT HAS TO BE WITH ME?
TAFFY. SHHH. KEEP QUIET, GIRL. DON'T WANNA WAKE UP THE OTHER GUESTS. WHAT'S GOT YOU ALL RILED UP?
GRRRRR!
CHANCES ARE, IF YOU'RE IN A POSITION OF POWER OR CELEBRITY, AND YOU HAVE SOMETHING TO HIDE, IT'LL BE ON THE FRONT-PAGE NEWS EVEN-TUALLY. IT'S JUST A MATTER OF TIME.
HUH. WELL, WOULDJA LOOKIT THAT?
PETRA GAVE ME THE RUNDOWN, BABY. I KNOW WHAT YOU NEED, JUST WHAT YOU LIKE. AND WHEN IT'S ALL DONE, WELL, I AIN'T NEVER LAID EYES ON YOU BEFORE.
GOOD GIRL.
HEH. YOU SEE THAT, TAFFY? I GUESS IT'S TRUE WHAT THEY SAY. POLITICS MAKES STRANGE BEDFELLOWS.
THIS'LL KEEP YOU IN MILK BONES FOR A YEAR, GIRL.

ONLY A MATTER OF TIME.
I LIKE CANDLES. THE FLAMES. THE WAY THE LIGHT FALLS ON YOUR BODY.
BUT DON'T GET TO THINKING I'M A HOPELESS ROMANTIC. WHAT I LIKE BEST ABOUT THEM IS THE WAX, AND THE WAY IT BURNS.
YOU CAN HAVE ANYTHING YOU WANT IN L.A. YOU CAN TEMPT FATE, LIVE DANGEROUSLY, WALK THE RAZOR'S EDGE...BUT ONLY FOR SO LONG.
ANYTHING YOU WANT, BABY.
THE THING ABOUT PLAYING WITH FIRE, THOUGH? YOU'RE BOUND TO GET BURNED.
I CAN'T WAIT TO GET A TASTE OF YOU, GIRL.
TRUST ME. THE FEELING'S MUTUAL.
ONE WAY OR ANOTHER.

KERASH
STA
F AL HO
CRUNCH
"OOH, THIS'LL BE THE PERFECT PLACE TO HIDE."
"WE'LL BE ABLE TO RAID THE OTHER FUNERAL HOMES AND CEMETERIES IN THE CITY. NOBODY'LL EVER LOOK FOR US HERE!"
SHUT UP, THE TWO OF YOU! I DIDN'T HEAR ANY-ONE COMING UP WITH A BETTER PLAN.
I HAVE A BETTER PLAN. IN THIS ONE, I KILL YOU ALL, AND THEN I DON'T HAVE TO LISTEN TO YOU BICKER.
EXCELLENT PLAN. PARTICULARLY SINCE IT WILL MEAN THE PEOPLE OF LOS ANGELES WILL NO LONGER HAVE TO FEAR THE BONES OF THEIR DEPARTED LOVED ONES BEING GNAWED UPON BY GHOULS.
WHICH IS SECOND ONLY TO THE WHOLE MICHAEL DOUGLAS/ CATHERINE ZETA-JONES THING ON THE EEEW-METER.

KILL HIM, YOU FOOLS!
YEAH, KILL ME! YOU CAN DO IT.

OR MAYBE YOU CAN'T.
KRAK
COME ON. YOU CAN DO BETTER THAN THAT!
YOU GUYS AREN'T EVEN TRY-ING.
AIEEE!

IT'S OT FAIR. REALLY SN'T.
HAT LONG-IRED GIRL OKED QUITE ESHY. I HAD HOPED TO SUCK THE MARROW ROM HER BONES.

WAIT, DID HE JUST CALL ME FLESHY? FLESHY?? I SPEND TWENTY HOURS A WEEK AT THE GYM, AND I'M FLESHY??
KILL HIM.
KINDA THE PLAN.

DIEE!

SPLURTCH
OH, MY. THAT IS SIMPLY REVOLTING.
NO KIDDING. I MEAN, I'M THE ONE HE SAID WAS FLESHY. WHAT'S WITH ANGEL? DOES HE SEEM ALL TESTY TO YOU? Y'KNOW, BROODIER THAN USUAL.

OKAY, GROSS. AND THAT SAID, WHAT'S UP WITH YOU TONIGHT?
NOT THAT THOSE GUYS DIDN'T DESERVE "THE WORKS," BUT YOU SEEMED A LITTLE MORE ENTHUSIASTIC THAN USUAL.

IT'S A SEX THING, ISN'T IT? I CAN TELL --I'VE CAUSED MY SHARE OF FRUSTRATION. AND, WHOA, ONCE IN A HUNDRED YEARS ISN'T EXACTLY BATTING A THOUSAND.
CORDELIA!

REALLY, IT ISN'T EVEN BATTING-- OOH, I'M BEING PUNISHED FOR MY INSENSITIVITY, AREN'T I?
AAHH!

I.
HATE.
THIS.

ANOTHER VISION?
AND A MIGRAINE THE SIZE OF TEXAS. THANKS FOR CARING.
KINDA THE VARIETY PACK OF PROPHETIC VISIONS THIS TIME. A NAME, A PLACE, A FEMALE VAMPIRE, AND THEN JUST...

"...FIRE.

"I RECOGNIZED THE VICTIM'S NAME, TOO. JACK CHARLES. HE'S A CONGRESSMAN OR SOMETHING."

WELL, TAFFY HERE WAS THE ONE SPOTTED HIM IN THE FIRST PLACE.
GOT A NOSE FOR SCANDAL, THIS PUP. OUGHTTA HAVE HER OWN SHOW.

NGRESSMAN D A HOOKER TH 'IM. ONLY ONE DY IN THE ROOM, THOUGH.
NO SIGN OF ANYONE IN THE CAR. SHE PROBABLY BROUGHT HER OWN RIDE.

JEEZ, FRANK, YA THINK THAT'S WHAT DID HIM IN?
HA HAHAHA HA
IS THAT RESPECTFUL? COME ON, GUYS. BESIDES, THE GUY LOOKS EXTRA CRISPY TO ME, NOT ORIGINAL RECIPE.

NOTHING MORE DECEPTIVE THAN THE OBVIOUS.

WHAT'S YOUR INTEREST IN THIS CASE? I DIDN'T THINK IT WAS YOUR KIND OF THING. OR IS POLITICAL SCANDAL ANOTHER OF YOUR HOBBIES?
NEVER REALL HAD TIME FO POLITICS. I HA WORD THAT THIS MURDER ISN'T WHAT IT SEEMS.
WHY MURDER? WE'VE GOT NOTHING TO INDICATE THAT AT THIS POINT. IT ISN'T MY CASE, IF YOU'VE GOT SOMETHING CONCRETE.
CALL IT A... HUNCH.
I WON'T DENY YOUR HUNCHES ARE USUALLY DEAD-ON. BUT UNLESS YOU CAN GIVE ME SOME-THING SOLID, THE INVES-TIGATING DETEC-TIVES WON'T WANT TO HEAR IT.
I'LL GE BACK T YOU.

ARE YOU CERTAIN YOU SHOULD BE DOING THIS, CORDELIA? I'M NOT SURE YOU'VE PROPERLY CONSIDERED THE DANGERS INVOLVED.

IT'S JUST A DATE, WESLEY. PEOPLE HAVE THEM ALL THE TIME.
WELL, PEOPLE WHO AREN'T YOU.

YES, WELL, I STILL THINK YOU OUGHT TO CONSIDER YOUR ACTIONS CAREFULLY. HOW MUCH DO YOU KNOW ABOUT THIS CHAD FELLOW, ANYWAY? WHAT ARE HIS INTENTIONS?
DINNER AND A MOVIE, WES. MOTIVATED BY LUST. WHICH, IF ALL GOES ACCOR-DING TO PLAN, SOUNDS JUST FINE BY ME.

HEY, CORDELIA. YOU READY? I HOPE YOU'RE HUNGRY. THE CHEF AT ARTURO'S HAS QUITE A REPUTATION. YOU WON'T BE ABLE TO GET ENOUGH.
THAT'S WHAT THEY ALL SAY.

SEE YA, WES. DON'T WAIT UP.

HMPH. WHY, THAT MAN COULD BE ONE OF THOSE FLY-BY-NIGHT TYPES. HE COULD BE A THRAGIAN INCUBUS FOR ALL SHE KNOWS.
OF COURSE, THE ANNOYANCE I'M CURRENTLY FEELING HAS ABSOLUTELY NOTHING TO DO WITH HOW LONG IT'S BEEN SINCE I'VE HAD A DATE.

"ON THE OTHER HAND...
LA COUNTY CITY MORGU
"...AT LEAST I'M NOT THE ONLY ONE."
EXCUSE ME.
YOU'RE NOT THE ONE I'M LOOKING FOR.
THERE YO ARE, CONGR MAN.
ZZZIIIPP

RACKLE
INTERESTING.

SO MUCH FOR THE CAUSE OF DEATH. YOU CAN'T GET PUNCTURE WOUNDS FROM A FIRE.
PARTICULARLY NOT ON THE INSIDE OF THE THIGH.

SLEEP WELL.

Arturo's
WELL, MY FATHER WANTED ME TO FOLLOW IN HIS FOOTSTEPS AND BECOME A PHARMACIST.
CAN YOU PICTURE IT? I MEAN, REALLY, ME? A PHARMACIST? HE COMPLETELY IGNORED MY LOVE FOR CARS. NOBODY KNOWS CARS LIKE I DO.
HELL, NOBODY SELLS CARS LIKE I DO.

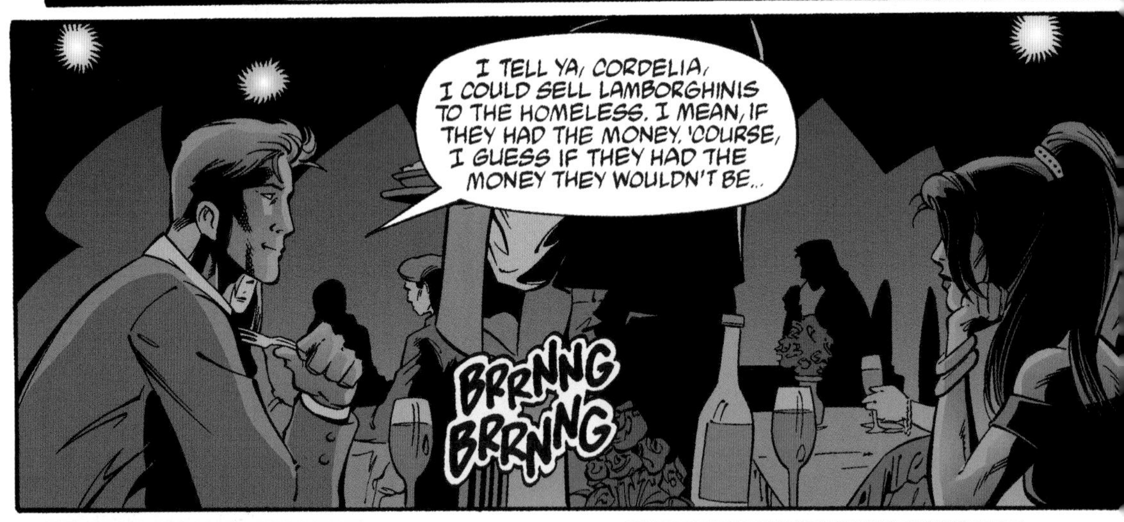
I TELL YA, CORDELIA, I COULD SELL LAMBORGHINIS TO THE HOMELESS. I MEAN, IF THEY HAD THE MONEY. 'COURSE, I GUESS IF THEY HAD THE MONEY THEY WOULDN'T BE...
BRRNNG BRRNNG

HOLD THAT THOUGHT, WILL YA, DOLL? THIS IS PROBABLY OLIVER. I'VE BEEN WORKING ON HIM TO BUY A LAMBORGHINI FOR MONTHS. JUST EXCUSE ME FOR ONE SECOND.

OR BETT YET, I CO JUST EXC YOU FO LIFE.

..I FEEL REAL WKWARD ABOUT HIS. IT'S MY FIRST ME, Y'KNOW, WITH...
IT'S JUST... MY WIFE'S BEEN SICK A WHILE AND... A MAN GETS LONELY.
DON'T WORRY ABOUT A THING, SUGAR. STICK WITH ME AND YOU'LL NEVER BE LONELY AGAIN.
QUICK, LET'S GET UPSTAIRS.
COME ON, SUGAR. LET'S SEE WHAT YOU'VE GOT.
OH, HONEY, IT'S ALL FOR YOU.
THINK THAT'S OUGH FOREPLAY. SIDES, I CAN'T TEN TO YOU YMORE. ARE OU EVEN STENING TO W STUPID YOU SOUND?
OH, YEAH BABY, I-- WHAT?
OH, JUST SHUT UP AND DIE.

NOW IS THAT ANY WAY TO TREAT A PAYING CUSTOMER?
KRASSH
BACK OFF, COWBOY. YOU DON'T KNOW WHAT YOU'RE MESSING WITH HERE.
I'M SORRY. I'M SORRY. CI ALWAYS SAID G WOULD PUNISH IF I STRAYE I GOTTA GO HOME
PROBABLY A GOOD IDEA.

WAIT A MINUTE. YOU'RE ANGEL, AREN'T YOU, MMM? YOU INTERRUPTED MY DINNER, HONEY, BUT AIN'T NO REASON WE CAN'T MOVE RIGHT ON TO DESSERT.
ARE YOU GOING FOR SEDUCTIVE? IT'S NOT WORKING.
ON THE OTHER HAND, JUST BEING NEAR YOU HAS ME THINKING ABOUT PENETRATION.
YOU DON'T KNOW WHAT YOU'RE MISSING, ANGEL.
I KNOW EXACTLY WHAT I'M *MISSING*. TRUST ME. YOU'RE NOT IT.
KEERASH
IT COULD'VE BEEN SO SWEET.

YOU WANT TO RUN?
RUN.
BUT YOU CAN'T FEED IN THIS CITY WITH-OUT ANSWERING TO ME.
KRAAK

YOU'RE NOT THE RST VAMPIRE CALL RL I'VE RUN INTO ATELY. ONE OF YOU LLED CONGRESS-AN CHARLES. I WANT NAMES.
HOW ANY OF YOU RE THERE? HO ARE YOU ORKING FOR? NSWERS, NOW, R YOU'LL BE ATCHING THE SUN RISE.
NOW, NOW, BIG BOY. YOU GOTTA PAY EXTRA FOR THE ROUGH STUFF.
SASHA. OH WOW. YOU COULDN'T HAVE COME AT A BETTER TIME. I'M SORRY ABOUT BEFORE. I SWEAR I'LL NEVER--
SHUT UP, CANDY. YOU GOT US IN ENOUGH TROUBLE. AND HERE WE ARE CLEANIN' UP YOUR MESS AGAIN.
NOW COME ON, HANDSOME. THIS WON'T TAKE BUT A MINUTE.
YEAH? MAYBE YOU'VE BEEN DOING IT WRONG.

Y, MY, BABY, OU'RE A BIG NE. ANY MORE KE YOU BACK HOME?
NO, THERE AREN'T ANY OTHERS LIKE ME.
AAARRGHH!
WE GOT NO LOVE FOR CANDY, BUT WE TAKE CARE OF OUR OWN.
NONE OF THIS IS YOUR CONCERN.
YOU SHOULDA KEPT YOUR NOSE OUT OF OUR BUSINESS.

!
A MAN IS DEAD. YOU'RE ALL KILLERS. THAT MAKES IT MY BUSINESS.
THANKS FOR THE SAVE GIRLS. BUT I GOTTA GO.
YOU'RE MAKING A MISTAKE. WE'RE HERE TO CLEAN UP A MESS, THAT'S ALL. WE DON'T WANT TROUBLE WITH YOU.
CANDY'S IN TROUBLE 'CAUSE SHE BROKE THE RULES. DREW TOO MUCH ATTENTION. JUST LET US BE ABOUT OUR BUSINESS AND...DAMN! SHE'S RABBITING.
I'LL SAY THIS FOR YOU HONEY, YOU SURE KNOW HOW TO SHOW A GIRL A GOOD TIME. BUT WE GOTTA CATCH UP WITH THAT GIRL OR WE'RE DUST.
KLANNG
UNGHHH!

WELL THAT WORKED OUT WELL.
I CAN JUST HEAR THEM NOW.
"YOU WERE FIGHTING HALF A DOZEN SCANTILY CLAD VAMPIRE HOOKERS IN A DARK ALLEY?
"NO WONDER YOU GOT DISTRACTED WITH ALL THAT FORBIDDEN FRUIT AROUND."

I WASN'T DISTRACTED, WESLEY. I WAS... OUTNUMBERED. HAVE YOU BEEN HERE ALL NIGHT?
THERE WERE A GREAT MANY BLADES THAT NEEDED SHARPENING. YOU REALLY MUST TAKE BETTER CARE OF YOUR TOOLS. BESIDES, I THOUGHT I SHOULD REMAIN IN CASE YOU NEEDED ME.
YOU REALLY DON'T HAVE ANY SOCIAL LIFE AT ALL, DO YOU?
THAT'S NOT VERY KIND. SOUNDS LIKE THE POT PITYING THE KETTLE IF YOU ASK ME.
SORRY, WES.
WE'VE BOTH HAD LONG NIGHTS, BUT I MAY HAVE JUST THE THING FOR YOU.
WHAT ARE YOUR FEELINGS ABOUT VAMPIRE HOOKERS?

"IT WAS A NIGHT TO REMEMBER, I'LL TELL YOU THAT. NOT THAT I'M THE KIND OF GIRL TO KISS AND TELL."
SURE, I COULD HAVE SPENT MY NIGHT HERE AT THE OFFICE MAKING THE WEAPONS ALL SHARP AND SHINY--BUT I HAVE A SOCIAL LIFE.
NOW SEE HERE! I HAPPEN TO HAVE A VERY ACTIVE SOCIAL LIFE. IN ACTUALITY, I TURNED DOWN A WONDERFUL OPPORTUNITY IN ORDER TO REMAIN HERE AND ATTEND TO THE ARMORY.
THE NUNS HAD TO GET SOMEONE ELSE TO CALL THE NUMBERS AT BINGO?
I'M GLAD YOU HAD SUCH A GOOD TIME LAST NIGHT, CORDELIA. WHAT DOES THIS GUY DO, ANYWAY? PRODUCER? DIRECTOR?
WHAT ARE YOU PLYING? FOR YOUR FORMATION, THE JERK AS A CAR SALESMAN, AND ABOUT AS APPEALING AS REGIS ON VIAGRA.
SO WHAT DID *YOU* DO LAST NIGHT, MR. CHASTITY?
STILL INVESTIGATING YOUR LAST VISION. CONGRESSMAN CHARLES WAS MURDERED BY A VAMPIRE, A PROSTITUTE NAMED *CANDY O.* THERE ARE LOTS MORE WHERE SHE CAME FROM.
OKAY, I FEEL BETTER ABOUT MY THRILLING DATE LAST NIGHT. A VAMPIRE WHOREHOUSE. BRRR. GLAD I'M NOT *THAT* DESPERATE.
I MEAN, THE WELL IS DRY, BUT AT LEAST I'M NOT DOING A RAIN DANCE.

LOOKS LIKE THIS ONE'S NOT AS CUT AND DRY AS WE THOUGHT, LOCKLEY. LIEUTENANT TOLD US TO RECRUIT SOME HELP. YOU WANT IN?

WHOA. BACK UP, JENKINS. I THOUGHT YOU GUYS HAD THAT PRETTY MUCH WRAPPED UP. WHAT HAPPENED?

AUTOPSY REPORT CAME IN. M.E. SAYS THE ESTEEMED CONGRESSMAN WAS DEAD BEFORE THE FIRE GOT TO HIM. GUY WAS EX...EX...
EXSANGUINATED. IT MEANS ALL THE BLOOD WAS DRAINED FROM HIS BODY.

I KNOW WHAT IT MEANS, PAUL. I'M NOT STUPID. ANYWAY, ALL THE GUY'S MAJOR BLOOD VESSELS WERE COL-LAPSED. STOPPED HIS HEART. NEVER A GOOD THING.

I'M IN.

ar des Anges
Anges
WELCOME
★tree-beard: tonight
WHAT THE HELL DO YOU WANT WITH ME NOW, BLONDIE?
IS THAT ANY WAY TO TREAT THE PERSON WHO GOT YOU OUT LAST TIME YOU WERE PICKED UP FOR SOLICITATION, LUISA? WE HAD A DEAL. YOU OWE ME.
SAY IT A LITTLE LOUDER, BLONDIE. THIS YOUR FIRST TIME WORKIN' WITH A SNITCH? 'CAUSE YOU SUCK AT IT. IF EVERYONE KNOWS I TALK TO YOU, THEY WON'T TALK TO ME.
NOW WHAT YOU WANT?
WHAT DO YOU KNOW ABOUT WORKING GIRLS IN THE FETISH SCENE?
WHAT KINDA FETISH, DETECTIVE? WE GET ALL KINDS.
BLOOD FETISH.
HELL, THAT'S EASY. MOST GIRLS WON'T RISK BLOOD GAMES. FREAKS LOOKIN' FOR THAT STUFF ONLY GOT ONE PLACE TO GO IN L.A. DYANNA ALLEGRA'S GIRLS, OUT IN SANTA MONICA.
YOU HEAR ANYTHING ELSE, YOU LET ME KNOW.
YOU'LL HEAR FROM ME, BLONDIE. WHATEVER I GOT, I SELL.

WELCOME, GENTLEMEN. CAN I HELP?
SOMETHING TELLS ME YOU CAN. WHAT WE'RE LOOKING FOR IS KIND OF UNUSUAL...
...JUST A LITTLE... BITE.
THEN YOU'VE COME TO THE RIGHT PLACE.
I HOPED YOU'D SAY THAT.
I THINK I'LL TAKE *YOU* MYSELF, HANDSOME. ACTUALLY WE'VE BEEN EXPECTING YOU ...ANGEL.
LOOKS LIKE THEY'RE ON TO US.
YES, WELL, THEY WOULD BE, WOULDN'T THEY? CORDELIA'S A BETTER ACTOR THAN YOU ARE.
NOW THAT'S JUST MEAN.

WE HEARD ALL ABOUT YOU FROM MIA AND JILLIAN. YOU KILLED SOME OF OUR FRIENDS, ANGEL. THEY HURT NO ONE AND YOU DUSTED THEM. WE OWE YOU.
YEAH, THEY WERE HARMLESS LITTLE CAMPFIRE GIRLS. I OWE YOU? FINE. I'LL GIVE YOU WHAT I GAVE THEM.
THAT WILL BE ENOUGH!
WELCOME, ANGEL. YOU WILL UNDERSTAND, I'M CERTAIN, THAT MY GIRLS ARE GRIEVING FOR THEIR LOST SISTERS. BUT WE UNDERSTAND YOUR HAND WAS FORCED.
THE BLAME FOR ALL OF THIS FALLS UPON MY PRODIGAL, CANDY O.
I HAVE EXPLAINED THAT TO YOU, GIRLS. AND YOU WILL ABIDE BY MY WISHES.
NOW I'M GOING TO HAVE A LITTLE CHAT WITH ANGEL. IN THE MEANTIME, SHOW HIS LITTLE FRIEND EVERY KINDNESS. DON'T HURT HIM...UNLESS, OF COURSE, HE ASKS.
REALLY, LADIES...YOU'RE ALL VERY LOVELY, BUT IT'S NOT NECESSARY. I'M REALLY RATHER... SEE HERE, I HAVE NO DIFFICULTY PROCURING MY OWN COMPANY AND... ANGEL!
YOU RELAX, HONEY. YOU DON'T NEED HIM. YOU GOT US ALL TO YOURSELF. IT'LL BE LIKE THE BEST DREAM YOU EVER HAD.

I GUESS I DON'T HAVE TO TELL YOU WHAT I'LL DO TO YOU IF ANY-THING HAPPENS TO HIM.
HE'LL BE FINE.
WOULD YOU LIKE A DRINK? ALL FROM WILLING DONORS, I ASSURE YOU.
I'LL PASS. A FEW WEEKS BACK, I CAUGHT ONE OF YOUR GIRLS DRAIN-ING A JOHN IN A PARKED CAR. I KILLED HER. NOW I'M HUNTING CANDY. VAMPIRES PREY ON HUMANS. I PREY ON VAMPIRES.
YOU TOLD THOSE GIRLS I WASN'T THEIR ENEMY. MAYBE YOU SHOULD EXPLAIN TO ME HOW THAT WORKS.
MY GIRLS DON'T KILL. SURE, THEY GIVE A LITTLE PAIN, EVEN TAKE A LITTLE TOO. BUT ONLY WITH CON-SENT, ONLY FOR PLEASURE.
THE MEN WHO COME HERE KNOW WHAT THEY WANT, AND WE GIVE IT TO THEM. EVERYBODY WINS. BUT NO-BODY DIES.
LIVE AND LET LIVE. BLEED AND LET BLEED. I'D THINK YOU'D UNDERSTAND. YOU FIGHT YOUR OWN URGES, DON'T YOU? WE'RE KINDRED SPIRITS, YOU AND I.
WHY DO I DOUBT THAT? YOU'RE SO BENEVOLENT, HOW DO YOU EXPLAIN CANDY?
SOME GIRLS CAN'T CONTROL THEMSELVES. THEY NEED THE DYING. WHEN THAT HAPPENS, THEY'RE NOT WELCOME HERE ANYMORE.
I'LL NEED CONVINCING.
I CAN DO THAT.

I WAS HOMECOMING QUEEN. I'M IN A CITY FILLED WITH GORGEOUS MEN. CAN THEY SENSE I'M FROM A SMALL TOWN? DO I HAVE SUNNYDALE COOTIES?
...DAMN SPOT... WHO NEEDS MEN ANYWAY? MAYBE ABSTINENCE ISN'T SO BAD? ANGEL MANAGES OKAY. AND WESLEY...OH GOD, WHAT AM I TALKING ABOUT?
CORDELIA CHASE CAN'T GET A DECENT DATE. IF THAT ISN'T A SIGN OF THE APOCALYPSE, I DON'T KNOW--
HI THERE. I'M JAY FARNHAM. MY LAW OFFICE IS NEXT DOOR? I GOT THIS PACKAGE FOR YOU GUYS BY MISTAKE. GLAD I CAUGHT SOMEONE IN. YOU'RE WORKING AWFULLY LATE.
LATE? YEAH. IT'S BEEN A VERY LONG, CATASTRO-PHICALLY BORING DAY, FILLED WITH DISENCHANTMENT.
BUT I'D SAY THINGS ARE LOOKING UP.

I KNEW YOU'D HAVE A HARD TIME BELIEVING ME, ANGEL. I AM NOT A FOOLISH WOMAN. I WON'T TRY TO TELL YOU I'M ANYTHING BUT WHAT YOU KNOW I AM.
BAD. SINFULLY SO. OUR KIND ARE MONSTERS, AND THERE'S NO ESCAPING THAT. BUT ALL I'VE TOLD YOU IS TRUE. WE'VE FOUND A WAY TO GET BY IN THIS WORLD.
I NEED TO EARN YOUR TRUST. AND I'M *MORE* THAN WILLING.
THAT'S ENOUGH OF THAT.
START EARNING. WHISPERING IN MY EAR BUYS YOU NOTHING. GIVE UP WHAT YOU'VE GOT ON CANDY O. THEN WE'LL SEE HOW MUCH I CAN TRUST YOU.
JUST LIKE THAT?
DON'T YOU WANT TO MAKE ME WORK A LITTLE HARDER AT THIS? MAKE IT LAST LONGER?
I'VE NEVER RUN ACROSS ONE LIKE YOU BEFORE.

NO. YOU HAVEN'T.
I'LL PLAY ALONG FOR THE MOMENT. IF I LEARN YOU'RE LYING ABOUT WHAT YOU DO HERE, I'LL TAKE THE WHOLE PLACE DOWN. DUST TO DUST.
IF THAT'S THE WAY IT HAS TO BE.
LATER, THOUGH, YOU'LL BE THINKING ABOUT ME. WHEN YOU DO, REMEMBER THIS. I KNOW ALL ABOUT YOU, ANGEL. IT MUST BE LONELY BETWEEN WORLDS.
CANDY'S REAL NAME WAS SHARON NUSSBAUM. RUNAWAY FROM BALTIMORE. BEFORE I FOUND HER, SHE WAS WITH A WEST HOLLYWOOD DEALER NAMED DEKE COSTAS.
NOW WE'RE GETTING SOME-WHERE.
JUST KEEP YOUR HEAD DOWN FOR A BIT NOW. CANDY KILLED A CONGRESSMAN. THE COPS ARE GOING TO NEED TO THROW THE MEDIA A BONE. YOU DON'T WANT IT TO BE YOU.

I'LL WORRY ABOUT THE POLICE. YOU FIND CANDY, AND LET HER KNOW SHE BROKE MY HEART. MIA AND JILLIAN WILL ACCOMPANY YOU.
I DON'T THINK SO.
WHAT'S THE MATTER, BABY, YOU AFRAID OF US?
YOU WANT TO COME ALONG, FEEL FREE. BUT SAY GOODBYE NOW, 'CAUSE YOU WON'T BE COMING BACK.
TOUGH GUY. YOU DON'T HAVE TO BE THAT WAY. BUT I THINK I UNDERSTAND WHY. YOU DON'T WANT US GETTING TOO CLOSE.
FINE, GO. REMEMBER WHAT I SAID, THOUGH. WHEN IT'S QUIET AND DARK.
YOU CAN'T GET WHAT YOU NEED ANYWHERE ELSE.
YOU HAVE NO IDEA WHAT I NEED.

I LIKE WHEN THEY BROOD.
NICE BUNS.
NOW GIRLS.
OH, ANGEL... THANK GOODNESS YOU'VE RETURNED.
I'VE GOT A LEAD ON CANDY. EX-BOYFRIEND. SHE MIGHT HAVE GONE TO HIM FOR A PLACE TO LIE LOW.
WONDERFUL. LET'S GO. QUICKLY.
BYE, WESLEY. COME AGAIN SOON.

YOU LOOK PRETTY WRECKED, WES. SHOULD I ASK WHAT HAPPENED BACK THERE?
IT WAS HORRIBLE, ANGEL. THEY TOOK MY STAKE.
ANGEL?
WE MEET IN THE STRANGEST PLACES.
IT'S NOT WHAT YOU THINK.
YOUR SOCIAL LIFE IS NO CONCERN OF MINE. RIGHT NOW MY ONLY CONCERN IS HOW JACK CHARLES GOT ALL THE BLOOD DRAINED OUT OF HIM, AND FINDING THE HOOKER WHO FLED THE SCENE.
WE NEED A BODY ON THIS, ANGEL. A FLESH AND BLOOD SUSPECT. PIXIE DUST WON'T DO. AM I GOING TO GET WHAT I NEED?
I'LL SEE WHAT I CAN DO.

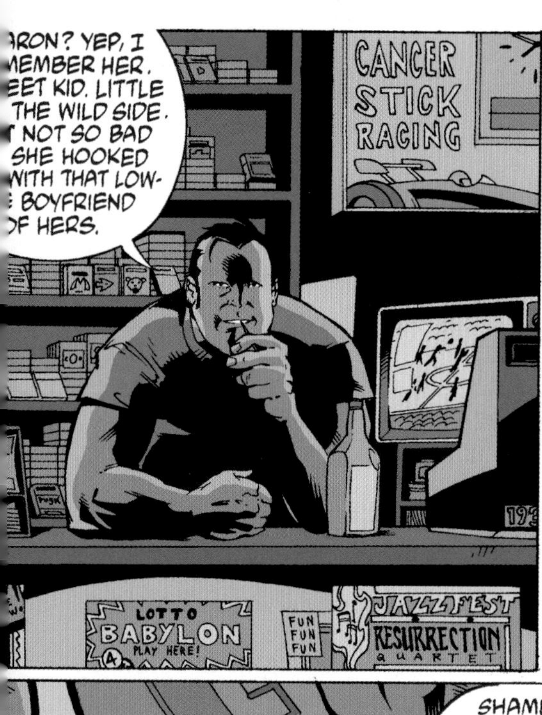
ARON? YEP, I MEMBER HER. EET KID. LITTLE THE WILD SIDE. T NOT SO BAD SHE HOOKED WITH THAT LOW- E BOYFRIEND OF HERS.
CANCER STICK RACING
LOTTO BABYLON PLAY HERE!
FUN FUN FUN
JAZZFEST
RESURRECTION QUARTET

WE'RE TALKING ABOUT DEKE COSTAS?
THAT'S HIM. HE'S THE ONE GOT HER ON THE JUNK, PUT HER ON THE STREET.
FUGS

SHAME, TOO. THOUGHT SHE'D GOT FREE OF THE SLEAZEBALL, THEN SHE SHOWED UP AGAIN.
WHERE CAN WE FIND THIS DEKE?
HELLO! GAS COMPANY. YOU HAVE A... UH... A LEAK. A GAS LEAK.
RAP
YEAH, YEAH. COME ON IN. IT AIN'T LOCKED.

HOLD ON. YOU AIN'T FROM THE GAS COMPANY.
YEAH? WHAT GAVE US AWAY?

WE'RE LOOKING FOR CANDY O.-- A.K.A. SHARON NUSSBAUM.
NEVER HEARD OF 'ER.
NOT VERY CONVINCING, DEKE. NOR VERY SMART. TRUST ME, YOU HAVE NO IDEA THE SORT OF CREATURE YOU'RE PROTECTING.

OH, HE KNOWS EXACTLY WHAT HE'S DOING. YOU TURNED HER, DIDN'T YOU?

DAMN RIGHT. THE LITTLE WITCH LOVED EVERY MINUTE OF IT.

I DON'T CARE ABOUT YOU, DEKE. I WANT CANDY. NOW.
WESLEY, GIVE ME A STAKE.
A STAKE. YES ...A STAKE.

NEVER LET IT BE SAID THAT I'M UNABLE TO IMPROVISE.

CANDY O. NOW.
SHE CAME BY LAST NIGHT. WANTED MONEY, CLOTHES. I EVEN GAVE HER SOME SMACK. OLD TIMES' SAKE. BUT SHE'S GONE, MAN. DUNNO WHERE.
I DON'T BELIEVE YOU, DEKE. THAT'S BAD FOR YOU.
OKAY, OKAY. GO TO THE U-STOR-IT OFF ALAMEDA. UNIT'S REGISTERED IN MY NAME. JUST DON'T TELL 'ER I TOLD YA. SHE'S NOT THE FORGIVING TYPE.
NOT GOING TO BE AN ISSUE.
NOoooOO

RAGE Nº 08
ORAGE Nº 10
UP
SKREEEK
KRUNCH
WHAT IS IT WITH THE RATS?
DON'T ASK. I HAVE A THING ABOUT RATS. LONG STORY.

WHY CAN'T YOU LEAVE ME ALONE?
YOU KILLED A UNITED STATES CONGRESSMAN. WHO KNOWS HOW MANY OTHERS. DON'T ASK FOOLISH QUESTION--
--UCKKK! DISGUSTING!
LET ME GO!
YOU'RE NOT LEAVING.
AHHHH!
I'VE GOT HER!

LIKE HELL YOU DO!
KRASHH
I TOLD YOU...
...YOU'RE NOT GOING ANYWHERE.
UP
UP
I'LL FINISH HER.
WAIT.

WE NEED HER ALIVE.
I'M STILL NOT SURE HOW THIS IS GOING TO WORK.
LAPD

IT'LL TAKE SOME SPIN CONTROL, BUT IF YOU TIME IT RIGHT, I THINK YOU'LL GET EXACTLY WHAT YOU NEED.

LOVELY TO HAVE MET YOU, LINDA. I WAS WONDERING...WOULD YOU LIKE TO GET OFF LATER...I MEAN, WOULD YOU LIKE TO GET TOGETHER WHEN YOU GET OFF... WORK, I MEAN WORK...
YOU KNOW, YOU'RE KINDA SWEET.

LISTEN, THINGS WERE AWKWARD EARLIER, BUT I WANT TO THANK YOU FOR YOUR HELP ON THIS.
I OWE YOU. AGAIN.

YOU DON'T OWE ME ANYTHING, KATE. THAT'S NOT THE WAY I WORK.

DETECTIVE JENKINS, HOW CERTAIN ARE YOU THAT SHARON NUSSBAUM IS THE WOMAN WHO KILLED CONGRESSMAN CHARLES?
ONE HUNDRED PERCENT. WE'VE GOT A WITNESS, AND A PARTIAL CONFESSION.
MISS NUSSBAUM!
MISS NUSSBAUM! DO YOU WANT TO MAKE A STATEMENT?
WHY'D YOU DO IT?
NOO! NOOO!
YOU DON'T UNDER-STAND! I CAN'T GO OUT THERE!
NOOOO!
HAVE YOU EVER HAD PSYCHIATRIC COUNSELING?
WHAT ARE YOU SO AFRAID OF, SHARON? HAVE THE POLICE BRUTALIZED YOU IN ANY WAY?
FWAAAASH
GOOD CHRIST!
FOR MY NEXT TRICK...

AN EXTRAORDINARY DEVELOPMENT, NEWS CAMERAS CAUGHT THE FIRST-EVER TELEVISED CASE OF SPONTANEOUS HUMAN COMBUSTION. AUTHORITIES ARE STILL DEBATING...
I LOVE IT WHEN A PLAN COMES TOGETHER.
BA-THUMP
WHAT ARE YOU DOING HERE?
I DIDN'T THINK YOU WERE HERE. I WAS WRITING YOU A MESSAGE...
NOW I CAN TELL YOU IN PERSON.
I WANTED TO THANK YOU FOR TRUSTING ME. YOU WON'T REGRET IT. I ALSO WANTED TO--
I THINK YOU SHOULD GO.

THAT, ON THE OTHER HAND, YOU WILL REGRET. YOU TAKE CARE OF YOURSELF, ANGEL. I'LL BE THINKING OF YOU. IN THOSE QUIET TIMES.

COMING UP NEXT, THE WEATHER, WITH TRISH CAMPBELL. IT'S GONNA BE A HOT ONE, BOYS AND GIRLS. MORE ON THAT, RIGHT AFTER--
KLIKK

"I KNOW ALL ABOUT YOU, ANGEL.

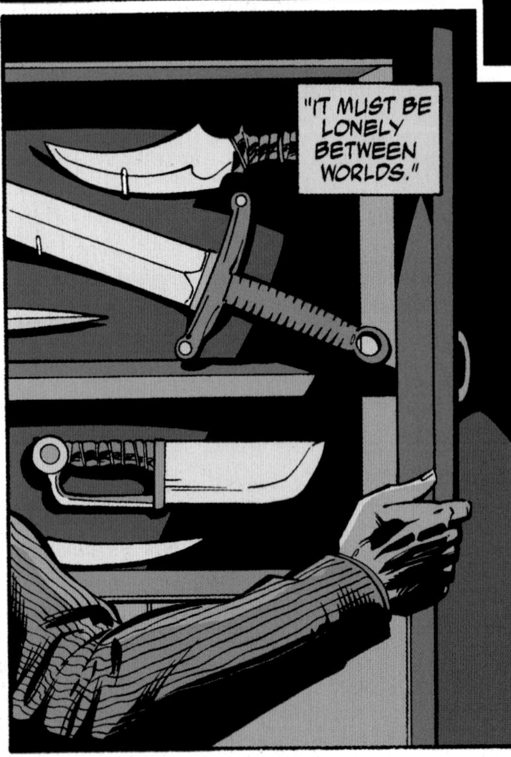
"IT MUST BE LONELY BETWEEN WORLDS."

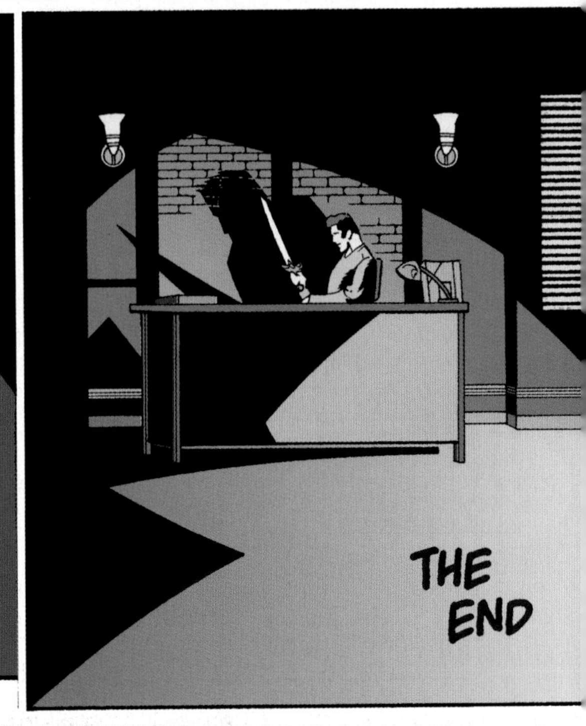
THE END

ANGEL™

PHANTOM DENNIS

story
CHRISTOPHER GOLDEN
& TOM SNIEGOSKI

Art
ERIC POWELL

letters
PAT BROSSEAU

colors
LEE LOUGHRIDGE

Eric Powell
with Lee
Loughridge

LOS ANGELES, CALIFORNIA. THE APARTMENT OF CORDELIA CHASE.
FOR THE LAST TIME, LUCY, YOU CAN'T BE IN DE SHOW!

WAAAAHHHH

OF COURSE, CORDELIA ISN'T THE ONLY PERSON WHO LIVES HERE.

ALL RIGHT... MAYBE "LIVES" IS A BAD CHOICE OF WORDS.
CLICK
CLICK

WESLEY, CHECK THE WINDOWS. SEE IF ANYONE FOLLOWED US.
NOT THAT I'M UNSYMPATHETIC ABOUT THE OFFICE, Y'KNOW, BLOWING UP ...BUT I STILL WOULD RATHER HAVE FOUND ANOTHER PLACE TO HIDE THE THING-THE-DEMON-HORDES-WOULD-HAPPILY-KILL-ME-FOR.
IT WASN'T REALLY A CHOICE, CORDELIA. THEY KNOW WHERE MY APARTMENT IS. CERTAINLY, KEEPING IT HERE IS AN INCONVENIENCE...
...BUT SUSPEC THE OUT COME--T APOCALYP --WOULD EVEN MO BOTHER SOME.
IT ISN'T FOREVER, CORDELIA. JUST TONIGHT. UNTIL WE CAN MAKE SURE THIS DEMON SECT IS PUT DOWN FOR GOOD.
FINE. >SIGH< WHY IS IT ALWAYS THE APOCALYPSE? AND LOOK AT ME! I'M FILTHY!

WHA...OH, THANKS, DENNIS. NICE TO SEE ONE OF THE MEN IN MY LIFE CAN STILL BE THOUGHTFUL. BUT I DON'T THINK A FACECLOTH IS GOING TO DO IT.
I NEED A HOT BATH AND LOTS OF SCRUBBING.

PRIORITIES, CORDELIA. YOU MIGHT WANT TO HIDE THE JAR BEFORE YOU BEGIN THE HOT SCRUBBING... THE BATHING OF YOUR...RIGHT. PRIORITIES.
IF THE HEART OF JONNAS IS RETURNED TO THE DEMON'S CHEST, HE'LL BE ABLE TO COMMAND ALL THE DEMONS STILL ON EARTH.
AND THEN THEY WON'T BE LURKING IN THE SHADOWS ANYMORE. THEY'LL BE AN ARMY.
AN ARMY. RIGHT. I GET IT. NOW CAN YOU GUYS JUST GO AND WIPE THE DEMONS OUT ALREADY?
MY FEET ARE KILLING ME.
THANKS, DENNIS. YOU'RE SO SWEET.
WHY ARE ALL THE GOOD ONES MARRIED OR DEAD?

LOCK IT UP GOOD. DON'T ORDER PIZZA. DON'T OPEN IT FOR THE LANDLORD. DON'T OPEN IT FOR ANYONE UNTIL WE COME BACK.
ENJOY THE SCRUBBING.

YEAH, GREAT. AND IF YOU DON'T COME BACK, THE OLD DEMON-HEART-IN-THE-JAR WILL MAKE A HECK OF A CONVERSATION PIECE...OR A DOOR-STOP. WILL YOU *GO* ALREADY?

C'MON, DENNIS. YOU HEARD THE BOYS. PUT YOUR NICK-AT-NITE ADDICTION ON HOLD FOR TEN MINUTES AND HELP ME FIGURE OUT THE BEST PLACE TO HIDE THE EVIL ORGAN.
TV GUIDE

LET'S THINK. IF I WAS AN EVIL ORGAN, WHERE WOULD I WANT TO BE STASHED?

I KNOW, NOT MUCH IMAGINATION ON MY PART. AT LEAST IF I ONLY USE ONE HIDING PLACE, I WON'T FORGET WHERE THIS STUFF IS.
I NEED TO TALK WITH ANGEL, THOUGH. NO MORE ARCANE ARTIFACTS MIXED WITH MY UNMEN-TIONABLES. WE NEED A NEW OFFICE.

ALL RIGHT. NOW WE JUST HAVE TO HOLD THE FORT UNTIL ANGEL AND WESLEY GET BACK.

I DON'T SUPPOSE THE PHONE RANG WHILE I WAS OUT? I WAS SURE I WAS GOING TO GET A CALL BACK ON THAT SHOWTIME SERIES.
TV

YOU HAVE *NO* MESSAGES.
STORY OF MY LIFE. ALL RIGHT, TIME FOR THAT BATH NOW.

NOW, NO PEEKING. JUST BECAUSE YOU'RE A GHOST, DON'T THINK I DON'T KNOW WHEN YOU'RE THERE.
TV

ONE LONG, HOT BUBBLE BATH LATER...
WHAT IS THIS MALE OBSESSION WITH THE REMOTE? IT'S LIKE, YOU'RE DEAD, AND YOU STILL HAVE TO BE IN CONTROL. MEN.
CHIP?
SEE, THAT'S THE PROBLEM WITH TECHNOLOGY, DENNIS. IT COMPLICATES LIFE WITH MORE BILLS. YOU'RE LUCKY. THEY DIDN'T EVEN HAVE CABLE BACK WHEN YOU WERE STILL ALIVE.
Y'KNOW, I'M NOT EVEN HUNGRY. I KNOW SNACKS ARE FROM THE DEVIL. AND YET SOMETIMES...
...CHOCOLATE CHIP COOKIES ARE WORTH A FEW EXTRA HOURS AT THE GYM.
I AM A PRISONER IN AN EGG FOO YUNG FACTORY.
SCRITCH SCRITCH

ALL RIGHT, WHO'S THE SMART ALECK WITCH. YOU OWE ME ONE EGG.
I HARDLY THINK THAT'S A PROPER WAY TO ADDRESS ONE'S FATHER.
DADDY, I'M SORRY.
I THOUGHT IT WAS MOTHER, OR SERENA. I'D HARDLY EXPECT YOU TO--
CLICK!
HUH?

WHAT THE--?

KRAKK
UHNGHH!

OOUFFF!
ALL RIGHT. NOW YOU'RE IN TROUBLE.

YOU'VE GONE AND MADE ME MAD!

SLAM!
HUNHH? WHAT'S... WHAT IS... DENNIS? HOW DID I...

DENNIS, I'VE TOLD YOU A MILLION TIMES. IF I FALL ASLEEP IN FRONT OF THE TV, YOU DON'T HAVE TO PUT ME TO BED... UNLESS...ARE YOU WATCHING THE SPICE CHANNEL AGAIN?
HEY, WHAT'S... LOCKED?

DENNIS! OPEN THIS DOOR RIGHT NOW! WHAT'S GOING ON OUT THERE?

GHOSTS. I HATE GHOSTS. ARROGANT BUNCH, THE LOT OF YOU. THINK I CAN'T HURT YOU 'CAUSE I CAN'T SEE YOU?

THINK AGAIN.

THUNKK
YAAHHHH!
OH, YOU ARE SO DEAD!
WAIT... WAIT A MINUTE--
KRASH

WHAT WAS THAT? I HEARD SOME-THING SMASH! THAT BETTER NOT HAVE BEEN MY MOTHER'S VASE! IT WAS THE ONLY THING I SAVED FROM THE I.R.S.

WELL, NOW YOU'VE COME TO YOUR SENSES AT LEAST.

DENNIS?

ALL RIGHT.
WHERE'S THE HEART?

HEY! DENNIS, LET GO! DENNIS!

SLAM
DENNIS!
DON'T LET HIM BREAK ANYTHING ELSE!
JUST BACK OFF GHOST-BOY. DON EVEN WANNA TOU YOUR LITTLE GIRL FRIEND. I JUST WA THE HEART. YOU CA TELL ME WHERE I IS, BUT SHE CAN.
BOOKS AND PICTURES?
THAT THE BEST YOU CAN DO?
WHAT ARE WE, GETTIN' A DIVORCE?
THAT LAMP AIN'T GONNA DO YOU ANY BETTER.

CLINKLE

ZZZZAPP
YEAAIIEEE!

A SIMPLE JOB, THEY SAID.
PICK UP THE HEART, BRING IT BACK, YOUR DEBT'S CLEAN.
IT WAS JUST BUSINESS.

IT AIN'T JUST BUSINESS ANYMORE.

KRASH

THAT'S IT! I WASN'T GONNA HURT THE GIRL BEFORE, BUT NOW--SHE'S *TOAST!*

COME AND GET ME, THEN. I'M READY!

KEEP HITTIN' ME AS MUCH AS YOU WANT, SPOOKY! BUT I'LL KEEP COMIN' BACK, AND ALL YOU CAN DO IS WATCH!
IT'S ALL OVER, NOW! IT'S ALL MINE. THE GIRL, THE HEART, AND EVERYTHING!

HA! I'
IN! NO
WHERE
THE HEA
YOU STU
BIMBO?

BIMBO?
I'LL GET TO YOU, GIRL. BUT FIRST...
AHA! IN THERE! THE HEART!
KRAK
HUNH?
YOU DON'T GET TO CALL ME A BIMBO UNLESS YOU KNOW ME FIRST.
AND... NOT EVEN THEN...
YOU KNOW WHAT I MEAN!

I TOLD YOU, BABE, I'LL BE WITH YOU IN A SECOND. THE HEART OF JONNAS FIRST...THEN YOUR HEART.
HEEEEYYYY!
YES! DENNIS! KICK HIS BUTT!
OOOFFF!

ALL RIGHT, LOOK...

THIS ISN'T EVEN MY FIGHT. IT'S A JOB FOR ME. ALL I WANT IS THE HEART.

LET ME JUST TAKE IT... AND I'LL BE OUT OF YOUR HAIR.

NO! DON'T YOU DARE OPEN THAT--!

OH, GOOD HIDING PLACE. NOBODY EVER THINKS OF THE *UNDERWEAR DRAWER*.

THERE YOU ARE, BABY. COME TO POPPA!

UNGGHH!

THIS IS WHAT YOU GET FOR PUTTING YOUR SLIMY DEMON HANDS ON MY FRILLIES!
DO YOU HAVE ANY IDEA HOW MUCH I HATE DOING LAUNDRY?
SPROINGG

?

AH, FOR CHRISSAKES!
I MEAN... AH, YOU KNOW WHAT I MEAN!
WATCH THE HANDS!

COME BACK HERE WITH THAT!

AH, GEEZ...

I'VE HAD JUST ABOUT ENOUGH OF THIS GUY.

THUNN

KEEP HIM DOWN, DENNIS! I'LL TAKE CARE OF HIM!

DENNIS? WHAT THE HELL KIND OF NAME FOR A GHOST IS "DENNIS"?
OH... OH NO...

...I SHOULDA JUST STAYED IN BED.

BONG

LATER...
CORDELIA? HOW WAS YOUR NIGHT?

SAME OLD, SAME OLD. HOW 'BOUT YOU GUYS?

ANGEL MADE SHORT WORK OF THE DEMON SECT, AND WE MANAGED TO SET THE CORPSE OF JONNAS ABLAZE.
THE HEART'S USELESS NOW.

PEACHY.

ARE YOU SURE YOU'RE ALL RIGHT, CORDELIA? YOU SEEM A LITTLE OFF. YOU DIDN'T HAVE ANY TROU-BLE WHILE WE WERE GONE?

NOTHING WE COULDN'T HANDLE.

POINT OF ORDER

story
DAVID FURY

Art
RYAN SOOK

letters
AMADOR CISNEROS

colors
DAVE STEWART

ANGEL™
EATED BY JOSS WHEDON AND DAVID GREENWALT
POINT OF ORDER
DAVID FURY AND RYAN SOOK
TH DAVE STEWART
E'S NOT ONLY SAVING SOULS ON TV--BUFFY'S EX IS
LSO BATTLING DEMONS IN A NEW MONTHLY COMIC.
ERE'S AN EXCLUSIVE ADVENTURE, CREATED BY
ARK HORSE COMICS ESPECIALLY FOR
TV GUIDE ULTIMATE CABLE READERS.
BANG
BA
BANG
ORDER! ONE AT A TIME!

THIS VIGILANTE IS A MENACE!
STREET FIGHTS--BACK-ALLEY AMBUSHES--IT'S LIKE THE OLD WEST OUT THERE.
YEAH!
TELL 'EM!

I USED TO FEEL SAFE GOING OUT AT NIGHT. BUT NOW--
WE WANNA KNOW WHAT YOU'RE DOIN' ABOUT THIS GUY!
YEAH!

AS YET, THIS SO-CALLED LANTE HAS ELUDED NY EFFORT TO... D OUR STREETS OF HIM.
BUT WE'RE GETTING CLOSE--
CLOSE?!

HE'S A CONSTANT DANGER TO THE COMMUNITY--LURKING OUT THERE EVERY NIGHT--AND YOU DON'T EVEN KNOW HIS NAME...
ANGEL.

THE NAME IS ANGEL.
>GASP<
IT'S HIM...

SO... YOU'RE THE ONE WREAKING HAVOC IN OUR CITY.
INTERESTING PERSPECTIVE. HERE'S *MINE*...

SEE, I'M NEW TO L.A. SPENT THE LAST FEW YEARS IN A QUIET LITTLE TOWN CALLED SUNNYDALE... MAYBE YOU'VE HEARD OF IT.
GOT ITS VERY OWN HELLMOUTH AND EVERYTHING.

ANYWAY, I'VE GOT THIS... PURPO NOW. TO ATONE-- REDEEM MYSELF FO SOME PRETTY NAST THINGS I'VE DONE. HELP PEOPLE. SOMETIMES THEY COME TO ME..

...SOMETIMES MY FRIEND DOYLE HERE LEADS ME TO THEM. HE GETS THESE VISIONS.
LONG STORY.

THE GIST OF IT IS, I FIGHT EVIL. IN WHATEVER FORM IT TAKES.
WHETHER IT'S ON THE STREETS... OR DOWN HERE, BENEATH THEM.

OH, ONE MORE THING...

I ALSO HAPPEN TO BE--

--A VAMPIRE.

AND I'M GOING TO KILL EVERY ONE OF YOU.

FLOOF
FLOOF
FLOOF

DESTROY HI-- UUGGH!
THUNK

PFFFT
SSSSSSSSSS

SHUNK

WELL ... IF THERE ARE NO OTHER ORDERS OF BUSINESS...
NOT ME.
I'M GOOD.

MEETING ADJOURNED.
A WHOLE RANGE OF *ANGEL* AND *BUFFY THE VAMPIRE SLAYER* GRAPHIC NOVELS ARE AVAILABLE FROM TITAN BOOKS.
the end

Stake out these Angel and Buffy the Vampire Slayer trade paperbacks

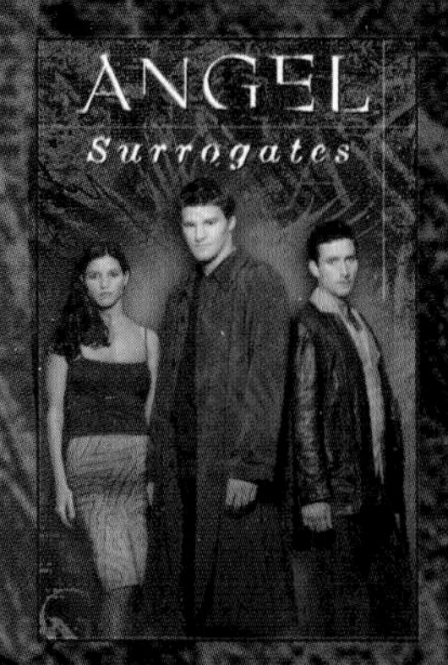

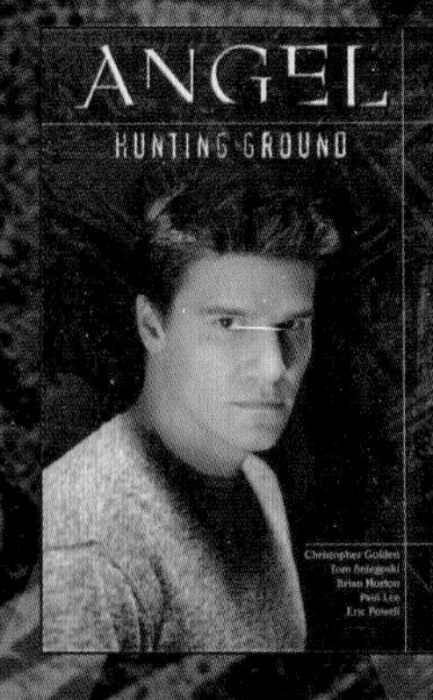

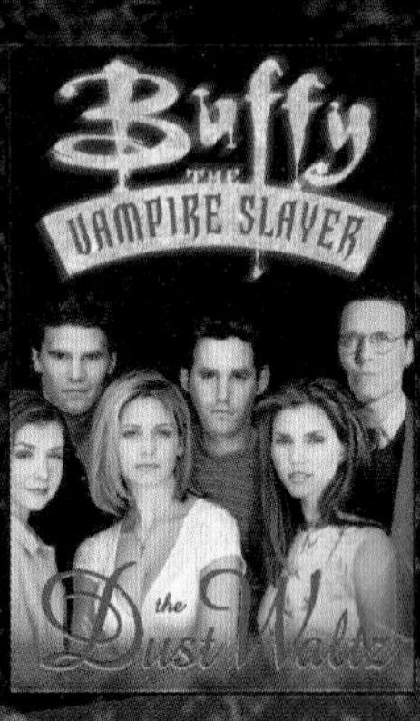

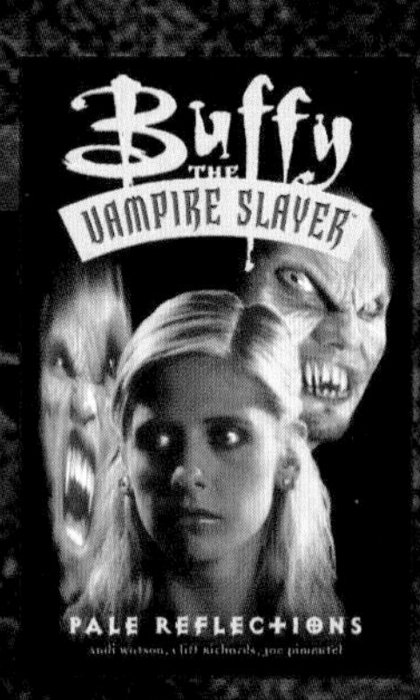

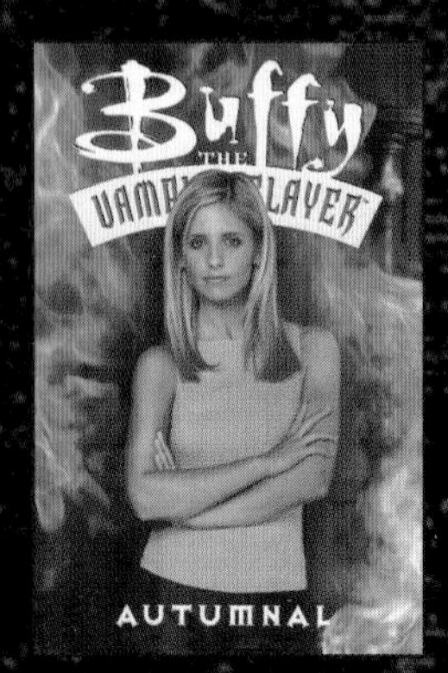